LOCKED OUT

RETURNING TO NORMAL

LOCKED OUT

RETURNING TO NORMAL

PATRICK JONES

darbycreek

MINNEAPOLIS

Darby Creek
A division of Lerner Publishing Group, Inc.
241 First Avenue North
Minneapolis, MN 55401 USA

For reading levels and more information, look up this title at
www.lernerbooks.com.

The images in this book are used with the permission of: © iStockphoto.com/
Imagesbybarbara (young man); © iStockphoto.com/DaydreamsGirl (stone);
© Maxriesgo/Dreamstime.com (prison wall) © Clearviewstock/Dreamstime.
com, (prison cell).

Main body text set in Janson Text LT Std 12/17.5.
Typeface provided by Adobe Systems.

Library of Congress Cataloging-in-Publication Data

Jones, Patrick, 1961–
        Returning to normal / by Patrick Jones.
            pages   cm. — (Locked out)
        Summary: When Xavier's father returns to Boston after serving ten
    years in federal prison, tensions quickly mount and Xavier's anger explodes
    on the baseball field, making it less likely that he will achieve his dream of
    playing in the major leagues than that he will follow his father's path.
        ISBN 978–1–4677–5799–7 (lib. bdg. : alk. paper)
        ISBN 978–1–4677–6183–3 (eBook)
        [1. Anger—Fiction. 2. Fathers and sons—Fiction. 3. Baseball—Fiction.
    4. Conduct of life—Fiction. 5. Boston (Mass.)—Fiction.] I. Title.
    PZ7.J7242Ret 2015
    [Fic]—dc23   2014018199

Manufactured in the United States of America
1 – SB – 12/31/14

To Jessica Snow and the youth outreach team
at Boston Public Library, and students at
Judge John J. Connelly Youth Center
—P.J.

1.

"Xavier, great way to close out the game, son." Coach Baldwin gives a pat across the numbers on my back. The casual slap doesn't hurt at all, but what he says almost knocks the wind out of me. It's been a long time—almost ten years— since a man's called me son.

"Thanks, Coach!" I slam my fist into my glove in a sideways victory punch. A few of the other guys punch my arms in congrats as they walk by.

Coach Baldwin waits til they pass. "You've earned the role of closer."

"Thanks for trusting me not to blow it."

"You got to earn trust on the field and off it. Know what I mean?" Coach gives me a look.

I nod, glancing at my uniform. Red and white for the Charlestown High Townies. It's an ugly uniform, but not the ugliest I've ever worn. The blue and gray one at Eliot Juvenile Detention Center was definitely worse.

Coach Baldwin and my counselor, Mr. Big, are about the only ones who still believe in me since I got in trouble. Mom doesn't trust me, and Dad, well, I don't know a thing about him anymore.

"Great game, X-man," Marcus says, bumping my fist. He watches games from the bench.

"We'll celebrate after," I whisper. Coach has his rules, but we've got our own set.

Marcus starts laughing, which always cracks me up. He's making jokes the entire time we walk from the field to the cramped locker room. As soon as I get to my locker, I pull out my phone and text Jennie, hoping we can hook up later tonight. It'll be like winning a double header.

As I peel off my uniform and head for the shower, the fog of steam coming from the shower room makes it seem like I'm in a dream. I stand naked for a second and I think *it can't get any better than this.* And I know I'm right because come Tuesday, everything's going to change. Just like a closer comes into a game late to make the save, on Tuesday, Dad's coming home in time for my last few years of school. I just wonder if he'll make the save or blow it.

2.

"Xavier, you were screaming in your sleep again last night," Mom says softly.

I'm dressed sharp for school, gulping the hot black coffee in front of me while my mom sips cold tea. I wonder if the night screams were as loud as the wailing sirens and roaring voices of my nightmares.

"More bad dreams?"

"No." I fix her with a hard stare; she blinks, all scared, and looks away, but won't shut up.

As mom rambles on, I scroll through messages, check scores on ESPN, and text Jennie.

4

She's a girl from St. Agnes I hooked up with for the first time last month, during spring break. I like that she isn't getting clingy. I got no time for attachments. "Xavier, do you want to talk? I know you're under a lot of pressure with your—"

"I said, no."

She looks away and inspects her chewed-down nails. A text from Jennie flashes on my phone. I reply with words she won't be hearing at her Catholic high school today. Mom's questions feel like a hammer against my sleep-deprived skull. But when Marcus picks me up, we'll blunt that pain before school.

"Xavier, I'm scared too." Mom bites down on the bottom of her chapped lip until it bleeds.

I finish the coffee in two swallows, and then balance the white cup in my right hand. It doesn't weigh much more than the baseball I'll pitch at practice later today. "I'm not scared."

"Like I said—" Mom goes on. I wish I had a mute button for her mouth.

I close my eyes and imagine I'm on the mound. I cock my left arm and hurl the cup from the tiny kitchen against the apartment's heavy front door. The cup hits and breaks right below the ugly "Welcome Home" sign mom bought at Dollar Tree. Dad's coming home tomorrow to this mess he created and then left behind ten years ago: a frightened wife and an angry son.

3.

"Xavier, wake-up!" Marcus hisses and kicks me under my desk. English 10 equals nap-time, especially since I rarely get much sleep at home, thanks to the nightmares.

"Marcus, shut up." I kick him back, harder than I should for my best friend.

"Is there a problem?" Miss Williams asks like she doesn't know. I'm always the problem.

"No. Zero. Zip. Nothing," I answer, which cracks Marcus up. Miss Williams, not at all.

She does this little head shake thing and then goes back to talking about nothing I care about in the least, which could be most any of my classes. I'm borderline in all of them, lucky that Coach Baldwin is also Mr. Baldwin, my history teacher. We have an understanding that my grades in his class reflect my earned run average. If I'm pitching well, I get A's. Not, then D's.

"You wanna hit the club tomorrow, X-man?" Marcus asks. The club is what Marcus calls the basement room at his crib. He lives with his grams. She lives upstairs and isn't always aware, so he comes and goes, drinks and smokes whatever as he pleases.

"No. Big day, remember?" I remind him yet again of the countdown clock in my head.

"That's right, your dad's coming home." He fakes a smile. He knows that I won't hang with him as much once Dad's home. "What's the homecoming celebration, strippers and such?"

I burst out laughing, earning another nasty stare from Miss Williams. "I don't think so."

"Then what?" If there was a party, I wouldn't need to tell Marcus. He sniffs 'em out.

I don't answer, and not because I'm getting

the Williams evil-eye routine. I don't really know what's going to happen. I've imagined how the conversation should go. I've thought about the moment so often—when I'll see Dad in person for the first time in over ten years—that it's almost like it's already happened. Like when the memory of a dream feels real. Tomorrow we'll see if it's really a dream coming true.

4.

As practice ends, I jog over to Coach. He's wearing the same old red Charlestown High School windbreaker he wears every day. They'll bury him in that thing.

"Xavier, what do you need?" Mr. Baldwin asks.

"I have something going on at home tomorrow," I start, looking at the ground in front of me. "I was wondering if I could miss practice. Just this once."

He pauses, and I'm dying a little with each second of silence. I don't want to let him down.

He saw something in me, letting me pitch varsity as a ninth grader. With one hand patting me on the back and one foot kicking me in the butt, Mr. Baldwin almost always knows the right thing to say to bring out the best in me. "Get your throwing in at lunch," he finally says. "I'll find my catcher's mitt. Although, with your control so far this season, I might need a lion tamer's net."

I break out a phony laugh. "Good one, skip."

As I head toward the locker room, I jog slowly past the bleachers. Not many people come to see our games—hardly any students, fewer parents, almost zero dads. Lots of guys on the team don't have a dad at home. They're either dead or took off. I guess my dad's somewhere in the middle.

Ten years ago, my dad got locked up. It wasn't his first time. I'd visited him when he was in county jail, before, or so he said in one of his letters. I don't remember it. But then he got busted on fed drug trafficking charges, and that's ten years mandatory. He ended up in a federal pen in the middle of nowhere, Texas, while we're here in Boston with no way to visit. Not that he wanted me to "see him that way," whatever that means. We wrote letters at first, but I ran out stuff to say, and he did too. It's too expensive to call, so he's been as good as dead for six years. But tomorrow I'll see him and we'll start making up for lost time. I got a list of a thousand things to tell him, a hundred things to show him, fifty of my friends I want him to meet, and one thing he's got to witness: me on the mound, throwing smoke, saving the game.

5.

"Xavier, just be patient," Mom says. What she's really thinking is *"you've waited ten years, you can wait one more hour."* Except Dad should've been home by now. Where is he?

Dad told Mom he didn't want us to wait at the station. He figured the bus would be late coming in. He'd taken the bus from Dallas to Kansas City to Chicago to NYC. I look it up on my phone and see the bus pulled into the Boston station two hours ago, but he hasn't called. I wonder if he even remembers our number or how to use a phone.

"I'm sure he'll call any minute," Mom says, trying to convince herself. It's a sad little welcome home party. Half the people Dad used to know are inside. The other half are outside, but like Dad, they're felons, and Mom says that means they can't hang together. Same for relatives—it would be a felon family reunion. My two older half-brothers, Leroy and Gus, from Dad's first marriage, got popped the same time as Dad. Except they fought back. The gun charges, along with the drug rap, kicked their mandatory sentences to thirty years. Gus is in Ohio, while Leroy's down south someplace. I lost track and lost touch. And I just don't care about them much.

"Maybe something happened to the bus?" I suggest. I don't tell Mom the bus arrived on time.

"Maybe." She gives a reassuring smile that I see right through.

"Maybe it's best not to know everything," I say, what we should've said long ago. The edge of Mom's mouth twitches like she's trying not to react. "Like me getting locked up at

Eliot. Like you and Uncle Jake." I use finger quotes when I say "uncle." He's a family friend, but since Dad's been gone, he was more than a friend to Mom. I saw his wrinkled, naked butt too many mornings.

"I think it's best we just try to start over," Mom says. "The past is the past. I'm sure your Dad feels the same way. It's time for a fresh start as a family. A fresh start that—"

"That is ten years and two hours too late," I say as I rip down the welcome home banner.

6.

"Xavier, it's time for school." Mom yells from outside my locked door. My eyes ache in the May morning sunlight. After midnight passed with no sign of Dad, I texted Marcus. He swiped his grandma's ride and we drove around for a while. When I snuck in around three, I saw an empty wine bottle in the trash and Mom's door closed. There was noise, but not snoring.

"Let me sleep," I shout back way too loud, making my head hurt. "Leave me alone."

"Don't you have a game today?" Mom asks. Coach's rule is you can't play if you don't go to class. Since I'm his stopper, I better get myself together. I'll sleepwalk through school.

I stand up and almost lose my balance when the realization hits me: *Dad's home, at last.* "Is Dad awake?" I ask. Mom doesn't answer, and she's gone from my door when I open it. As I head into the bathroom, I see that Mom's door is still closed, and there are tiny hairs in the sink. Dad's. I take a quick shower to shock my system, throw on new threads, and head for the kitchen. The smell of coffee fills the air, but mainly it's the big smile on Mom's face that fills the small room.

"He said he's sorry," Mom says as she hands me a cup of hot, black coffee.

"What happened?" I blow on the coffee to cool it, and I remember Dad doing the same.

She starts telling me a story about Dad seeing an old friend. Lie. He's got none around here. The more she talks, it's like the less she believes it. Her smile fades with each word. I interrupt to remind her about my game. "How about Dad? Do you think you two—"

"I'll ask him," Mom says. "I'm sure he'll be

there if he can, but your father has lots of important things to do right away. Make appointments, find a job . . . You understand, right?"

I say yes, following up her lie with my own. I gulp my coffee to keep me from talking and asking more dumb questions with dumber answers.

7.

"Xavier, sit down please," says the school counselor, Mr. Big. His real name is Mr. Bigatoni, but since he's five foot four, he's Mr. Big. Other people make fun of him, but he's always been square with me. Especially after I got out of Eliot.

"Yes, sir." I sit in a chair older than I am; that's most of Charlestown High's furniture.

"Miss Williams says you were sleeping in class on Monday." He's got his glasses resting on his shiny bald head as he reads from a paper

19

in his hand. "She says it's not the first time."

"It ain't my fault she's so boring," I crack, but I get no reaction from Mr. Big.

"You can't sleep in class." We should change his nickname to Mr. Obvious. "Besides, if it was just her class, then maybe you'd have a point. But other teachers, other times. What's wrong?"

I don't tell him that I have nightmares at home, but when I sleep at school, everything's calm.

"My dad's home." I don't need to tell him from where. Everybody knows. I don't brag about my dad doing time, like some guys do, but I don't deny it either. And I know it's in my file someplace.

"Well, I'm glad to hear that." Mr. Big puts down the paper. "Maybe now you can get serious about school. If you want to play pro ball, you'll need to graduate from high school."

I smile. "'cause I'll need to know math to count up all my millions."

I can tell he's trying to stay serious. "I hope all your dreams come true. So, what are you going to do differently?"

"Start drinking more coffee."

He cracks a smile. "If there's anything I can do, you let me know, but you need to stay awake. Okay?"

"I feel you, Mr. Big." We do an awkward fist bump and I start heading to Miss Snitch's class. Nobody likes a snitch, which is why I know the story about Dad meeting a friend last night is a lie. Snitches got no friends.

.

"Xavier, you look like a fire hydrant!" Tio Hudson yells at me as I walk toward the team bus with Marcus. Tio's buddies crack up, but we just keep walking. He's right: the Townie road baseball uniforms got way too much red, even for my skinny self.

He walks over toward me and I feel myself tense up. He's smaller but harder than me.

"You been back to Eliot?" Tio asks. I'm not sure why he's talking to me.

"No, you?"

Tio looks me over as he considers his answer.

Unlike Tio, who's been in and out of Eliot many times, I only spent a few days. All my stuff was things that shouldn't even be crimes, like staying out too late, smoking weed, and other garbage that don't hurt nobody but me.

The way Tio talks to me, acting all tough 'cause he got popped, makes me feel like I'm a fire hydrant and he's a dog. "What's the next uniform you wearing? Burger King?" Tio laughs. He and his friends tease everybody who went to this summer job fair in March.

"Maybe," I mumble.

"If you want to make some real money, you come see me," Tio says.

"Everything okay? Xavier, Marcus?" Coach Baldwin just stepped off the bus. He's got this angry tone that suggests he's not happy with us talking to Tio. "Get on the bus. Mr. Hudson, you get stepping."

Tio laughs and mumbles something foul out of the side of his mouth about Coach Baldwin.

"Knock it off, Tio," I say. Tio gives me a hard look but walks back to his buddies. Funny, he's cracking on me for wearing a uniform when he and his banger buddies all look alike, dressed the same from head to tat to toe. "Come on, Marcus, let's get ready to blow smoke," I say as I head to the bus.

As we climb on, Marcus says, "You know going to Eliot don't make you tough."

"What does it make me?" I ask.

"It means you got caught," he says. "It either makes you stupid or a lousy criminal."

9.

"Xavier, you just need one more out." My catcher, Ryan, pats my butt to fire me up, but I don't need any more motivation than a simple glance at the stands behind our bench. There's a few moms, a few girlfriends, and a grandpa or two, but no fathers. There's nothing like dead-beat dads to inspire us to be better.

"I got this." I pound the ball hard into my glove. First guy took strike three for the KO, and the second hit a weak grounder to me. I personally tagged him out. We're ahead 4–1, and it's the bottom of their lineup. Mark up a

W for the Townies and an SV for the X-man.

The opposing catcher waddles to the plate. He looks like he's spent more time pigging out at Hong Kong Buffet than squatting behind the plate. Still, he's got power, hitting two long doubles in the game. Ryan puts down the sign. Fastball, strike one.

He fouls off another pitch that's fast but high, and then he lets one go that's faster, but too low. Ryan calls for a splitter, which I learned last summer at a baseball camp that Mr. Baldwin paid for. It's a hard pitch to control, but I snap my wrist tight, and he fights it off—foul.

"I thought you threw hard," the fat batter shouts. "My grandma throws harder than you."

I yell back about his mom, and he yells trash about my mom and dad. I'm steaming now; he's going to get burned. Ryan calls for a change, which is the right pitch. I shake him off and hurl smoke, high, inside—at the guy's head. He hits the dirt like a two hundred pound turd.

In an instant, we're both halfway between the mound and the plate. I hear Coach yelling, "Cool it!" but I don't care. I'm too pissed about what I didn't hear: my dad yelling from the crowd, *"Come on, son, strike this guy out!"*

I get the KO, except this time it's a knock-out, not the box score. It's going to be hard for him to talk trash again with a busted-up mouth. Coach Baldwin pulls me off the guy. The ump ejects me and then I'm in his face, cursing him out. I'm ready to cold cock the ump when Coach Baldwin wraps his arms around me. Coach gets the save this game, not me.

10.

"Xavier, what was that?" Coach Baldwin leans into me. He's got me sitting alone at the front of the bus like I'm in solitary in prison. That was when I lost touch with Dad in fifth grade, when he did three months in the hole.

"I own the inside of the plate," I tell Coach. He doesn't seem convinced that I made a baseball related decision and not just another angry, impulsive move.

"You're sitting the first game on Saturday," he says. "Think about what you did."

I act all remorseful when he walks away.

Soon as he's out of sight, I pull out my phone and text Jennie. We go back and forth, pretty hot and heavy. But I hide the phone when I hear somebody coming toward the front of the bus. The rest of the team is steaming mad at me. Normally the rule is we can be on our phones after a win, but Coach is punishing the whole team for me getting ejected. "X-man, what the hell was that?" Marcus whispers from behind.

"Nobody talks trash about my family," I whisper back.

"Except you," he replies, and I stifle a laugh. He goes back to join the team. It gets pretty loud and I hear Coach join in the conversation, so I pull my phone out, dip my head and call home. When there's no answer, I try Mom's cell. It goes to voice mail. I text Jennie again about when we can hook up next, but then a call comes in from Mom. I sink deeper in the seat.

"We're on the bus back. Is Dad home?" I whisper, even though I feel like screaming.

"No, not tonight, Xavier."

"Where is he?"

There's a pause. A long pause. "Out."

"You picking me up from school or do I gotta take the T?"

Another long pause. It's like I'm calling the moon instead of Charlestown. "The T."

"What's going on, Mom?" There's no answer. "I'll see you soon, Xavier."

Then my phone shows the call ended. I bury the phone and my anger in my pocket and look out the window at all the people in Boston who should be happy that they're not me.

11.

"Xavier, is that you?" Mom asks, like she doesn't know. Who else is going to be walking in our door?

I throw my bag, bat, glove, and spikes by the front door. "Is Dad avoiding me?" I ask.

She doesn't answer as I breeze past her like a fastball. I grab leftover Chinese food, which wasn't here this morning, from the fridge and open it up. "That's your dad's food," Mom says.

I close the sweet-and-sour-smelling carton and put it back. "Then where is he?"

"Out." Is that going to be her answer every time I ask?

31

Instead of Chinese, I make myself two bologna sandwiches. Mom and I don't talk while I slap some bread and deli meat together. Finally, just as I take a bite, she starts. "Xavier, you have to understand, for ten years he's been locked up, not able to come and go as he pleases. Having to eat whatever food they served, always having to answer to someone. Give him a few days."

I nod. It makes sense. "I have a game Saturday, a double header at Cambridge. I won't pitch in the first game." I don't tell her why. "But probably will in the second. It's Saturday, so you two could—"

Mom's lips tighten. If I don't ask them to come, they can't say no. She answers by cleaning the already clean kitchen. I chew, text Jennie, and stare at the door. It doesn't open. I tell Jennie to meet me at the Fenway T station in an hour. "I'm leaving."

"You just got home." Mom breaks her silence routine. "Don't you have homework?"

I answer by leaving the table, and fixing to meet Jennie. I get myself sharp, smelling fine, and ready to roll. Mom's standing by the front door, arms crossed and frown unmatched.

"Xavier, I'm sure your father will be home soon. You should wait for him, please."

I turn my Townie cap backwards so I can get closer to her face. I can smell that she's sneaking smokes. "You need to stay here," she says as I walk past her. "Where are you going?"

Just before I slam the door loud enough to wake the dead, I hiss one word. "Out."

12.

"Xavier, here's your coffee." Mom puts the cup on the table. I open up a breakfast bar and go to throw the wrapper away. I jam it in the now-empty Chinese food carton on top.

"Where were you last night?"

I rolled in around three again; their door was shut again. I ignore the question by putting in my earbuds. I see my bag's still by the front door, so I open it, pull out my math book and notebook, click the calc app on my phone, and act all studious at the kitchen table.

"You can't just come and go like you please."

I turn the music up louder.

"There will be consequences," I think she says. I'm trying to lose myself in the rhymes so I don't have to hear her telling me what I can and can't do. "Xavier, listen to me!"

She pulls the bud out of my right ear, but I put it back in. We do this dance a couple times before I let her know with a cutting, cold stare that I'm done with it. And her.

The buds go back in my ears as she walks away. I struggle through the first problem—like I need to know any of this stuff. So I close the book and I'm looking up scores when I feel mom's hand on my back. I almost jump, 'cause I don't like nobody touching me like that.

"What the f—" I start when the touch turns into a heavy hand. I turn around, and there's Dad standing behind me, all six-foot-three of him. When I hug him, it's clear he's still got some height on me.

He doesn't say a word or make a sound. I have to sniff loudly to hold the snot in as my eyes suddenly well up.

"Stop crying like a baby!" Dad lets go of the

hug. "Your mom told me 'bout you leaving when she told you to stay last night. You disobey me, little man, and I'll knock you across the room. You get me?"

He doesn't need to hit me—his tone just slapped the taste out of my mouth.

"I said, you get me?" His voice is different than I recall, like he swallowed sandpaper.

"I get you," I mumble.

"I get you, *sir,*" he says. I nod and for the first time in ten-plus years, I see Dad's smile.

13.

"Xavier, get me more crab legs!" Dad yells as I start toward the buffet line again. Mom looks happy to see him enjoying it all. For a lean guy, my dad can sure put away the Chinese food. He's on his fourth plate and fifth beer.

I don't remember Dad drinking this much before, but then again, I don't remember much about him. What I do remember, I get confused with my dreams and nightmares.

The line for crab legs is long, but I manage to get the last four. I pile more eggs rolls on another plate and head back to the table. Dad's talking to the waiter. Make that six beers.

Dad takes the plate. He doesn't offer the legs. "Sorry 'bout the game. I got busy."

"With what?" I ask. Mostly Dad's been asking us about people he used to know.

"You want a list, little man?" Dad cracks one of the claws. Juice flies across the table. "You my probation officer? I got to answer to you and to him and your mom. I just spent ten years explaining every move I make." He dips the meat in the butter and lets it rest for long time.

"Xavier, what your father means is that—" Mom cuts off as Dad fixes her with a stare.

"I don't need no translation service to talk to my son." He swallows the buttery meat. "I got to get a job, for starters. Then . . ." It's a symphony of cracking claws, gulps from a Bud bottle, and a bitter list of complaints. Pretty soon I'm sorry I asked; now he won't shut up.

"I understand," I say when he takes a breath to flag down the waiter for a seventh beer. "It's a long season. You'll get to a game."

"You any good?"

I nod.

"I never had time for no sports and such, too busy on the hustle." Dad tells war stories from back in the day without an ounce of regret in his voice. In his old letters, he talked about turning his life around, and I guessed I believed him. But back then I believed in Santa too.

14.

"Xavier, how you think I look?" Dad asks. We're at Goodwill buying him a suit for job interviews. Nothing seems to fit right. Like me, Dad's too tall and too skinny.

"Sharp," I say, mostly because I want to get out of here so I don't miss the team bus. I haven't asked Dad if he's coming to either of the games. "How about the blue one?"

"I ain't never wearing blue again," Dad says, laughs. It's a forced laugh, almost like he forgot how or something. "That's the only color I wore for ten years inside."

40

I nod and smile, but I'm not interested in hearing more about how tough it was for him on the inside, like anything I went through on the outside don't matter.

"Let's get me this suit," Dad says, motioning to the gray one he has on. "Then go start looking for jobs and get my PO off my back," he says.

Another nod. I've heard him on the phone talking to his probation officer. Dad already told his PO that he was looking for work. I wonder if lying to a PO is violating probation.

"I worked in the laundry first couple years, then the kitchen . . ." And it's prison story time again. I steal a glance at my phone, but Dad sees and he's not happy with it.

"What you doing with that? Seems like everybody's looking in their hands more than looking people in the eyes," Dad says. "Back in the day, when someone was talking to you, teaching you something, you'd look them in the eye and say 'yes, sir' and 'no, sir.' But I guess it ain't that way no more."

"You trying to teach me how to cook

oatmeal in prison?" I laugh; he doesn't.

"You got quite the mouth on you, little man," Dad says. I really wish he'd call me something other than "little man" since it implies he's a bigger man. "Come here!"

I pull myself off the chair and do as I'm told. He's got me standing next to him, looking into the mirror. He presses down the collar on the gray suit. "What you teaching me then?" I ask.

Dad turns from the mirror to look me in the eye. "Teaching you what *not* to do with your life."

15.

"Xavier, you're not concentrating!' Coach Baldwin is all flies on crap over me. He stands next to me on the sidelines as I warm up before the second game of our double header.

"I'm out of my groove." Jennie and friends are in the stands. Mom and Dad are not.

"Your grades at school aren't up to snuff, and not everybody wants you to play ball."

I don't ask, but I know Williams has an F next to my name.

"Is everything okay at home? Is something bothering you?" Coach asks.

43

I let it pass and attempt a confident stare. "I got this, Coach."

He shakes his head and jingles the keys in his pocket of his windbreaker. "Maybe I put too much on you, trying to make you a closer. I thought you were mature enough to handle—"

"You calling me a baby?" I shout. "I'm a grown-ass man, if you haven't noticed!"

"Lower your voice, Xavier." He goes to put his hand on my shoulder, but I move back.

I bang my left fist hard into my glove. The smack of the leather is one sweet sound. But Coach has had enough.

"Go grab some bench! When you're ready to listen and learn, we'll talk." Coach points at the dugout, but I don't move a muscle. I feel all tensed up like just before a 3-and-2 pitch.

"I won't tell you again." Don't he know by now that I take suggestions, not orders?

"I know you won't." I circle my left arm like I was getting it loose before a pitch.

He's in my face now, not a place anybody ever should be when I'm hot like this. Sometimes it's like the faucet broke and there's no way to stop the hot water from pouring out.

"Unless you want to get kicked off this team, you'll do what I say. You understand?"

I slip the glove off my right hand and crack my knuckles. Coach is talking at me, but it's as if I had my buds in my ears and I don't hear a word until he yells my name again. The sound that follows is a sour smack as I drop him like a bad habit with a right to the jaw.

16.

"Xavier, you going to play or what?"

I hold up my taped-up right hand to show the Eliot JDC gym teacher, Mr. G. At least it wasn't broken.

"Then run some laps, you can't just stand there!" Mr. G shouts.

"A'right, Mr. G." Typical Eliot garbage— if you're doing nothing, they yell at you to do something, then the other half of the time, they're yelling at you to stop doing something. We'd rather I was at school. By "we" I mean Mom, me, and the court appoint. Dad still

46

don't seem to care where I am, long as it's not in his way.

I start jogging nice and slow. This little guy with mean blue eyes and more tats than anybody that young should have runs beside me. "You not playing ball?" I ask the short guy.

"Nobody here can handle my game," he says. I can't tell if he's serious or not. Mr. G. yells at us to stop talking and run faster, so we half obey and pick up the pace. I ask him what he's in here for, and he starts telling stories way worse than I got. "How about you?" he asks.

"I punched out one of my teachers," I tell him. He doesn't look impressed, but since he's facing a weapons charge that don't surprise me none. "I don't know what's gonna happen with me. Just got to get back to the pitcher's mound."

"It's all about if they think you're a risk or not," he says. "If you've done time before, how serious the charge, how many times you lied to the judge, even if your old man did time."

"Really, about your father?" I whisper since we're passing Mr. G. "Why's that?"

"That's what a CO told me," he says. "He

47

says kids of criminals are a higher risk."

I run away fast as I can from the little guy with the big mouth. I work up a sweat, so I get permission to duck into the bathroom. I run cold water over my hot face and look in the smudged mirror. I take off my gray overshirt, the color of my dad's interview suit that hasn't landed him a job, and stare at the blue undershirt, just like dad's old prison uniform. Like father, like son.

17.

"Xavier, you got everything?" Mom asks as I walk out the double-lock door at Eliot. Not that I'm going free right away. They're gonna shackle me with an ankle bracelet like a slave.

I don't ask about why Dad ain't there. I didn't ask why he didn't visit me at Eliot. She drives me to school. "You're lucky they took you back. Thank Mr. Baldwin."

I'd kind of hoped he would've come to visit, but Eliot lets in family only. I wrote Coach a letter telling him how sorry I was for losing my cool and hitting him. He never wrote back.

These two and a half weeks were the longest time I spent inside, and I guess I understand now a little more what Dad went through, having every single thing you do controlled by somebody else. *Count off. Yes, sir. No, sir. Tuck in your shirt. Put away the book. Shut your mouth.* The COs at Eliot are order-giving machines.

"You got my phone?" I ask just before I head into school. Mom hands it to me. I text Marcus and then Jennie as I walk. For a second, I almost forget how my phone worked. It's like the rest of the world might've jumped ahead while I was stuck in Eliot.

I hit my locker at lunch. It's always interesting, the reaction people get once they've spent time at Eliot. Lots of guys in the life know you have to do time to prove yourself, mostly prove that you won't snitch. I get high fives from some, like Tio. But my locker neighbor and old teammate, Ryan, gives me nothing but a cold shoulder.

"You got a problem?" I ask Ryan when he turns his back on me and starts to walk away.

"Don't talk to me, Xavier." He turns around.

"Or to anybody else on the team, unless you make a public apology. But my guess is people like you don't know how to say you're sorry."

"People like me?" I clench my bruised fist. "What the hell does that mean, Ryan?"

He's shorter than me, but he's all high and mighty when he says, "Criminals."

18.

"Xavier, I accept your apology," Coach Baldwin says. We're in Mr. Big's office; I wonder if it's because Coach is scared to be alone in a room with me. Ryan might be right. Telling Coach I'm sorry was hard enough, I can't do it in front of the team. It'd be public snitching on myself.

"I just got angry, Coach," I explain. Maybe that's why the judge is sending me to anger classes.

"*Mr.* Baldwin," he says softly. "I'm not your coach anymore."

I try not to react, but that hurts. Being on the team mattered. Being on the mound mattered. Even if most of those guys weren't my friends, when we all wore the same jersey, I was part of something. Now, maybe the only uniform I'll ever wear is the blue shirt and grey sweats at Eliot.

"Thanks for letting me come back to school," I say to Mr. Big, who seems all in charge.

"It's not that simple," he starts talking about credits from Eliot. Sometimes he talks too much, like my lawyer did. I wince when he says "summer school."

"For sure?" I ask. Though I guess it might keep me out of trouble. I normally play city ball in the summer, but my ankle bracelet won't allow the travel.

"Even without this incident, you probably would have needed it in some classes," Mr. Big says. "Xavier, you've got to get serious about school if you want to have a future."

"And don't be talking about the big leagues yet," Mr. Baldwin says. "You've got the talent in your left arm, but you lack discipline in your life. Without discipline, you'll fail."

"We're happy to welcome you back here, so prove to us you belong," Mr. Big says.

I nod and look at the floor. It feels like I let these guys down.

"Now, you're off my baseball team—I don't have a choice," Mr. Baldwin says. "But you're still on *my* team. I'm still behind you Xavier."

"Thanks Coach—I mean Mr. Baldwin," I say. "So what summer school classes am I taking?"

This time Mr. Baldwin throws the first punch, not me. "English 10, with Miss Williams."

19.

"Xavier, would you like to share?" asks Miss Helm, the anger management leader. Do they get a lady who looks as good as her just so guys like me will come to the meetings? I'd share plenty with her, but I got nothing to tell anybody in this class.

"If you don't participate in the discussion, that's considering not attending. You weren't just sentenced to be here, but to make a unique contribution. Do you understand, Xavier?"

I fold my arms around me a little tighter, holding everything inside.

"I ain't got nothing to say right now," I mumble. "So I just contributed."

"We'll come back to you, Xavier." And then she moves on the next guy. He starts talking, but I'm tuning him out, trying not to stare at Miss Helm, trying not to think about the text Jennie sent me just before I had to come in here, and trying not to think about Dad. He's still just showing up in our family—he's not contributing. Might as well still be in Texas.

Guys keep talking and I end up listening in, although I don't know why I bother. It's not like they're saying anything different. I have no unique contribution because almost everybody in here is telling the same story. It's like the math story problems we get with too many parts. Start with a family. Subtract the father to the streets, prison, or grave. Add an overwhelmed single mom or overtired grandparent, and multiply that by fear, shame, guilt, and regret. What do you get? Rage.

"Xavier, what do you want to say?" Helm calls me out, which means time's almost up.

"Whose idea was it to force ten angry men

into a small room?" I ask. A couple guys laugh, which is better than crying, which it seemed like some of 'em might do. Miss Helm answers the question like lawyers, social workers, and probation officers do, with big words that have small meaning.

"When the sensation of anger approaches," she says, "inhale. Take a deep breath. Take as many as you can. Settle yourself. Look for tranquility inside. Resist the anger impulse."

I actually think that's good advice: I'll call Marcus and we'll inhale as many as we can.

20.

"Xavier, that's harsh," Marcus says when I show him the text from Jennie. She said she doesn't want see me again. She didn't say why. "What you gonna do?"

"I don't know," I answer. "She's hot and all, but she's been cold to me ever since Eliot."

"I bet it's her folks," Marcus says as he walks away from me. We're playing catch in the hallway of my apartment building with the door open so I stay in range of the ankle bracelet monitoring box. It's my last free day before summer school starts. "You know, even my

58

grandma, when she heard what you done, she had things to say."

"Like what?" I toss the ball his way.

"Said you were bad news and I best be staying away from you." The ball comes back.

"So why you here?" I throw the ball, harder, faster.

"'Cause you're my friend. Grandma can tell me some stuff, but not who my friends are," Marcus holds onto the ball. "You ought to tell Jennie that, about her parents."

"Good idea." I drop my glove, pull out my phone and call rather than text her. She doesn't pick up, so I leave a message saying just about the same thing. "What if she says no?" I ask Marcus after hanging up.

"She got anything of yours?"

"Last time we were together, before Eliot, I gave her my hoodie 'cause she was cold."

Marcus laughs. "That's it, tell her you want it back, and then you can hit her with some of your smooth X-man moves and lines when you meet up. Next thing you know, she'll be back in your arms."

"How'd you get so smart?" I put my glove back on and the ball comes my way.

"I used to watch my mom," he answers. "I saw how she kept getting tricked by players."

I look inside the apartment, where Dad's sleeping it off. Six weeks out of prison and he's still out of work, out of patience, but never out of beer or wine. I grip the ball tight and hurl it so hard that Marcus is shaking the hurt out of his hand as I turn and go back in.

21.

"Xavier, get out here!" Dad yells. I'm in my room struggling with a hard math problem. I'd ask him to help, but he doesn't have any more education than me. All that time in prison, I wonder why he didn't get a GED instead of just wasting time that he couldn't get back.

"What is it?" I shout back. He expects me to obey him like he's the CO at Eliot. Like I did inside, I take my sweet time walking out to the kitchen, making him wait. I got my phone in my hand in case Jennie calls. Dad's yelling about something, so I steal glances at my phone.

"Put that toy away!" Everything invented in the last ten years is a toy to him.

Just as I put it in my pocket, the phone buzzes. I steal a glance. Jennie. "I got to go."

"You're going nowhere, 'cept doing your homework and cleaning these dishes."

"I didn't dirty no dishes, that's you," I say. "Clean up your own mess."

"Listen, little man, I'm not your mother, you don't talk to me like that. You get me?"

I take a step forward. "What you gonna do? Hit me? If you do, guess what, I bet that's assault, and that violates your parole. Or how about that heater and stash you got? I don't think convicted felons supposed to be hiding guns and drugs under the sink. You get me?"

Dad's eyes light up with rage, maybe the first time I've seen them look anything but dead since he came out. "Shut your mouth, little man."

"I gotta take this," I pull the phone out and hold it up. "I'm out."

He says nothing as I head toward my room. I slam the door behind me and lock it. I listen to the message Jennie left. She's keeping the hoodie as a keepsake. Don't be mad, she says, like that's possible—anger class or no anger class. After the message, I hit up Marcus.

"Wassup?" he asks.

I tell him about Jennie's message, but not about my fight with Dad. "Marcus, come on over quick. I gotta see her." I look at the bracelet on my ankle. "And bring a set of pliers."

22.

"Xavier, your dad seems a'right," Marcus says as he walks into my room.

"You don't have to live with him." I motion for Marcus to sit. Normally we hang at his crib, but this bracelet won't let me go anywhere, do anything, or get in any trouble.

"Still." Marcus's dad died when he was young, then his mom just last year.

"You bring the pliers?" I ask Marcus. He looks away, so I know the answer is no.

"You sure about that, X-man?" He asks. I show him the bracelet. "It don't look so bad."

"That's 'cause you ain't wearing it. I'm all, beep beep on some jerk's computer screen."

"You're a live video game!" Marcus jokes, but I'm not laughing.

"It's stupid. Not like I can't do something wrong with this around my ankle."

Marcus walks over toward the window, looks outside. "You know how it works. It's to show the court that you can learn to follow the rules. What did you say it was? Thirty days?"

"Yeah. I guess, I know. Dad did ten years. I can do thirty days. I mean—" I'm interrupted by a loud knocking on the door.

"Xavier, open this door so I know what's going on in there," Dad shouts.

I don't move a muscle. Marcus walks from the window toward the door. "Don't!"

"I don't want no trouble," Marcus says. "You should do what your dad says, Xavier."

"Why's that?"

He looks as puzzled by the query as I do by math. "Because he's your dad, that's why."

More door pounding, but I can't make myself do what he tells me. For so long, I've been doing what I want. Now I'm supposed to listen to somebody that I don't respect, giving me orders.

Finally I motion for Marcus to open the door. Dad's right outside staring at me. He's nothing like the role model dad he's supposed to be, like I imagined, and like I need. Only way I know he's my dad is the same hot blood running through both of us.

23.

"Xavier Horton." Miss Williams calls my name. I grunt a response. I look around the room and it's an odd collection of athletes, bangers, and stoners. Mostly boys, only a few girls. Since I blew off the first day of this class as a power play, I'll have to get caught up on if they're single.

The teacher hands me a paperback book when I raise a hand, like a reward.

"Tio Hudson." She hands him a book too, like she has to everyone.

"I'm here, don't rub it in," he says. He gets a laugh, even from me at this hour, in the heat of this classroom. Even Eliot's got AC, but not Charlestown High.

Miss Williams fixes Tio with her evil eye, but he just makes a funny face in return. Tio hasn't hassled me since that one day 'cause I avoid him, but I think he's Marcus's kush connection.

As Miss Williams rambles on about her expectations, I turn to Tio. "Glad you're in here—this lady ain't got no sense of humor and—"

As if to prove my point, Miss Williams calls me out in front of everybody. "Mr. Horton, this is your second chance to succeed in this class." I grind my knuckles into the hard desk and take a couple deep breaths like they taught me at anger management class. "I hope you'll use this second chance wisely. Life rarely offers second chances, let alone third or fourth ones."

"How about fifth?" Tio asks. "I'll take a fifth of Bacardi 151." More laughter.

"Mr. Hudson, see me after class."

I turn around, fist-bump him and say, "You got a date on the first day." He laughs, but stops. He motions that Miss Williams is headed our way. She's over my desk like a dark cloud.

She leans in too close. "Let's not do this again. Let's try to learn from our mistakes."

I fiddle with the paperback, *The Red Badge of Courage*, on my desk. I don't look up at her. It seems learning from mistakes just ain't the Horton family tradition.

24.

"Xavier, answer your father," Mom says. We sit around a dinner of cheap frozen food. Since Dad came home, Mom lost her food stamps because he's a felon. And now we got to move, since this building is Section 8 and Dad's not allowed to live here. Dad asked me a question, but I couldn't understand him because he's slurring his words. "Tell him about school," Mom pushed.

I start reporting on summer school because Mom asked me and she don't ask much from me anymore. As mad as I was with Dad, I know chucking the bracelet would hurt me and Mom more than him. So I stay chained.

"Where you think that reading's gonna get you?" Dad says, or something like that.

"I'm gonna graduate from high school." I don't say "unlike you," but it's in the air.

"Then what? Get a job? Go to college? Let me show you something," Dad stumbles to his feet. Mom says he drinks more 'cause he's got a UA. If he uses drugs, it violates his parole. He can get drunk and angry on a bottle of wine, yell at me, and push my mom around. But he can't smoke a blunt and relax. Stupid. Sell weed, go away for ten years. Even stupider.

Mom motions for me to follow Dad as he walks, with the help of the wall, toward his room. He goes inside, but motions for me to stay outside. "Here's what happens when you got a felony drug charge." He slams the door. A few seconds later it opens again.

"You go to get a job." Slam goes the door.

"James, stop it, please," Mom yells from the other room. Dad ain't listening.

"So you think, I'll start a business, so you go to get a loan." Slam.

"Or go to school and learn a trade, but you need a loan." Slam.

"Or get out of this dump into a nicer building, but there's a background check." Slam.

"Or do anything just to be a man again, but no, this is what you get." Slam.

"They lock you inside, but then you get outside, and it's like you're still locked in." Slam goes the door, except this time it doesn't reopen. I walk back out, and Mom's crying. And so am I.

25.

"Xavier, how is your summer?" I laugh in my PO's face, maybe accidently spit on him.

"You got me shackled and drawn. How you think it is?" I ask him back. He gives off this salesman vibe with his fake smile, cheap suit, and golf trophies. He doesn't answer my question, but he expects me to answer his. So I just wait him out until he moves on.

"I see you're still attending anger management," he says, sounding bored now.

I nod but don't say nothing, just like in the

classes. All this talk hurts my head. Sometimes I wonder if Dad got tossed in the hole just to get away from all these people with power over his life—my life, our lives—talking at us like any of these words even matter. I nod some more, grunt an answer every now and then, and try to stay awake. It's hard to sleep at home with Mom and Dad always fighting, and no sweet thoughts of a girl in my life to ease me to sleep before the nightmares start.

"Anything else?" I ask. I keep peeking at my phone, hoping for Jennie. Nothing.

"Change is hard," my PO says. I think, *No, the lock on the bracelet, that's hard*. He starts giving me a pep talk like he's Coach Baldwin, but his words are empty. "Try harder, Xavier."

As I head for the T back home, I try calling and texting Jennie again, but again I get nothing. It's like I don't exist. But what I don't get is a picture she posted a few days ago. It's like eighty degrees, but in the pix, she's wearing my big hoodie. Is that her saying she hasn't forgotten me? When did I change from a man to a memory? And when did that happen with me and Dad?

26.

"Xavier, wait up!" Tio calls out after summer school.

I stop in my tracks. Tio's comedy act in school is the only good thing going so far this summer. Dad's no closer to a job, and Jennie's even further away. Last time I dialed her number, she'd changed it.

"What up?" I say when Tio catches up to me. He starts talking, cracking jokes about Miss Williams, making fun of the book we're reading and all that. He's a'right.

After a while, his voice gets quiet and

serious like he's telling a secret. "You were in Eliot again while back, right?" I nod; everybody knows. "You see a guy there we call Bubble? A little guy with an afro, squeaky voice, lots of tats, and cold blue eyes."

I nod. In the two weeks while lawyers argued about giving me serious time or the bracelet, I met a lot of guys at Eliot, though I avoided bangers like Bubble. "I saw him."

"He's out now. You know why?" Before I can answer, Tio continues, his voice even lower. "'Everybody heard 'cause he snitched. We want after him, but you know, they watching."

"So?"

"So you ain't connected, maybe you do me a solid and sometime down the line—"

I look away, mind racing. I've been running away from this kind of thing all my life, like a monster's chasing after me. I've seen the life eat up and spit out too many people. Like Dad.

"I get it," Tio says, then shrugs. "I shouldn't ask a son of snitch. I just thought—"

"Thought what." Now my low tone matches his.

"Thought you might want to join us. What else you got?"

I size him up and take stock. He's right: I got a dad who ain't one, a mom who tries but fails, no girl, no team, nothing 'cept a bracelet around my ankle keeping me chained up. I nod.

"You play baseball, right?" Tio asks. Another nod. "You gonna need your bat."

27.

"Xavier, what's your problem?" Dad shouts across the kitchen table.

The real answer is "you," but I don't say it. I just pick at my food and listen to music. He reaches for my buds.

"What's *your* problem?" I say, moving my head away. I glance at Mom. She's a wreck.

"What's my problem?" Dad stands and pounds the table with his left hand. "I tell you what my problem is, little man, it's everybody here on the outs treating me like I was still in."

Mom cuts in. "It's not fair, Xavier, he did his

time, and—" Dad shuts her up with a glare.

"I can't even visit my own sons, 'cause I'm a felon." Another table pound. "And my youngest son never even come to visit me." Now it's a Star Wars death ray glare right at me.

"You said you didn't want me to visit," I remind him. "Said you didn't want me to see—"

The next pound knocks the salt shaker on the floor. "You think I want you to see me like *this*? I can't do anything. Everything's closed. I did ten years that I can't get back, for what?"

"Why didn't you do more?" I'm thinking about Tio, Bubble, and my baseball bat.

Dad leans in, fists on the table, and right in my face. "What you saying, little man?"

"You got less time 'cause you snitched. That's all I'm saying."

He shakes his head back and forth so fast. "I didn't snitch on family. They had warrants on all of us. I would've done twenty if I hadn't given somebody else, somebody they would've got anyway. Then he gave somebody up, so I didn't need to testify—"

"Sounds like you're making excuses. You

need this." I flip him *The Red Badge of Courage*.

He looks at the book and then throws it across the room.

"James, calm—" Mom starts.

"I did ten, not twenty," Dad says. "You were five when the offer came. I thought if I took it, then I'd be out in time to watch my son grow up a little. But I guess that was a mistake."

Now I pound the table. The pepper falls. "You're good at those."

28.

"Xavier, don't do it."

Marcus and I sit in front of the TV watching the Red Sox. Mom's at work and Dad's "out." During a commercial, I told him about Tio, which means I guess I just snitched. Another round of like father, like son. Marcus passes me the blunt. I inhale deeply as the Red Sox score.

"Everybody thinks I'm a screw-up. Dad, Mom, Jennie, Coach, Mr. Big. Maybe you?"

"No, I just think stuff's really hard for you right now." He takes the blunt back.

"Sometimes I wish my dad never would've come home from prison and—"

Marcus cuts me off. "Don't say that. I'd kill to have my dad back. You got yours."

"No I didn't," I say. Getting this smoke in my system is making me feel light. "I got a stranger. For so long, I'd thought, maybe dreamed of how things would be when he got out, and nothing—and I mean nothing—is like how I thought. It's worse."

"X-man, that's harsh," Marcus says.

"I mean, Tio's right, I got nothing." I take the blunt back. "I just don't care."

"Man, listen to you." Marcus grabs the remote and mutes it. "You got baseball next year, maybe college ball too. Maybe your dad will work everything out. You gotta have hope."

"Just a setup for disappointment, is all this is," I say, my life as clear as the blue sky over Fenway.

"All what is?" Marcus asks.

"My dad's life," I say. "I don't want to be like him, but I know I am."

"That ain't no way to have hope," Marcus

says, shaking his head. He laughs. I don't.

"If I tell Tio no, he's gonna think I'm weak or a snitch like Dad," I explain. "I want to be better than my dad, harder, tougher, meaner. But if I do? Either story, I ain't no hero."

Marcus laughs. "Just 'cause you're not a hero, it don't make you a villain, Xavier."

29.

"Xavier, put that bat down!" Mom yells at me. Dad and I were into it again, about what I don't remember. I got up from the table and returned with a baseball bat. Why should I crack Bubble's skull, who ain't done anything to me, and not hurt the person who ruined my life instead?

The veins on Dad's skinny neck seem to be sticking up like two straws. "Little man, you'd better step lightly here." He very slowly fixes his eyes toward the sink and his heater.

"You ain't gonna do nothing!" I shout back. "You're just a coward. You read that book yet?

You learn anything? You learn anything about being a man? Being a father?"

"Just 'cause you busted up some coach don't make you a man, son," Dad says. The rare use of the word *son* jolts me. "A coward? I did ten long years in a federal pen. You think you're so tough 'cause you spent a few weeks in a kiddie jail. You don't know hard times, Xavier."

He holds my stare for a few long seconds.

"You think this is easy?" he asks me, but he looks at mom. "Every positive step I take forward, I get two boots in the butt backward. I'm trying to be a man, but nobody's treating me like one. I want to get a job, be a good father, raise my son right. But I don't know how."

"You ain't taught me nothing except how to fail!" I grab the bat so tight it hurts.

"What you gon' do?" Dad asks. "Smash my skull. Go ahead!"

"I might as well. You ain't gonna fight back, just like when they took you away from us."

Dad looks over at Mom, who's crying. "He doesn't know?" Dad asks Mom.

"I don't know what?" I shout. "A real man

would've fought back, but I guess you—"

"You know why I didn't fight back? Why I didn't shoot off a couple of rounds?"

"Maybe you were too afraid to have a gun in your hand," I say.

"When the police came, sirens blaring and screaming on a bullhorn to come out, I didn't have a gun in my hands." Dad's voice catches, and I'm stunned to see tears forming. "I had you in my arms, Xavier. I had you."

30.

"Xavier, come out of your room!" Dad pounds on my door. "Let's get going."

I pull the pillow against my head to drown out the sound.

"You're late for summer school!"

My head's a mess. Tired, still ringing from our shouts last night, confused. I remember Dad in the Goodwill saying he was trying to teach me how not to be like him. It seems like every day I'm turning into him anyway. But who is he? The man who did ten hard years for a life of crime, or the one who held me in his arms?

"I'm kicking it down if you ain't out here."

I leap from bed and throw the first kick to show I'm up. "At least I got someplace to go!"

"You think I ain't trying to get myself a real job?" He yells, still pounding. "Nobody wants me. How do you think it feels to be a grown man getting told that by everybody he meets?"

I know I'm supposed to yell, *I want you Dad!*, but I can't do it. "I wish you never would have come back here and messed everything up!"

Silence. Seconds later, the door explodes into the room, ripped off the frame with just one kick. Dad stares at me. He reaches back like he wants to punch me.

"James!" Mom shouts. I hear her shoes click as she runs toward him. Dad just stands there staring at me. Mom pulls hard on his left arm and he follows her, too easy.

Everything I thought I wanted, I got, and now I don't want it. What I thought life would be when Dad returned and what it's become are nothing alike. I step out of my room. I hear quiet sobs from the kitchen. I glance at Mom at the table, hand on Dad's shoulder. Real men cry too.

31.

"Xavier, where did you get these bills?"

Dad's holding the wad of cash in his big right hand; it must feel refreshing. "I sold your gun." I know better than to make eye contact 'cause I don't want to tell him who I sold it to (Tio). Word on the street is once a snitch, always a snitch.

I feel him breathing down my neck. "Why in the hell did you do that?"

Now I can look up. "To protect you. If you get caught, you're going back in. You gave up so much of your life already. If you're gonna

89

do wrong, then I got to make things right."

"Is that so?"

"I got something else for you too." I point at the kitchen table. "My PO let me walk around today and pick up job applications. I said they were for me, but I got them for you."

"Is that so?" Why is he repeating himself?

"I know you've had a hard time and I thought—"

He walks to the table and eyes the applications, picks one up, and wads it into a ball. He throws it at me, slower than my change-up. "I just got done wearing a uniform for ten years, and I'll be damned if I'm going wear another. Flipping burgers? Seriously? I used to be somebody."

"Used to be," I mumble. "I'm just trying to help after what you did for me."

He wads up and tosses another application. "I see what's going on here. Giving me money, telling me to get a job, acting all that, like you're the real man of the house. Is that it?"

I shake my head while he trashes the remaining applications. "Listen, you're still a little man until you done time in the big house like me. Two weeks in Eliot and a month in a bracelet don't make you nothing! It certainly don't make you the boss of me! You get me?"

He raises his hand but stops as I lean in, ready to take the blow like a real man.

32.

"Xavier, you still got it," Mr. Baldwin shouts as the ball smacks into his catcher's mitt. He saw me before school and asked if I wanted to throw for a few minutes.

"Thanks, Coach," I say. He doesn't correct me like he did last time I called him that.

"I hope I'll be your coach again, but that depends on you." He tosses the ball back my way. I catch it with my right hand. I bounce it up and down before moving it into my left to blow smoke.

"I won't let you down." I hurl a red hot rocket his way.

"But zero tolerance on the field, and you're going to have to keep your grades up on your own at school."

The ball comes back to me. I know it's not true, but it feels heavier after promising I won't let him down. Everything feels heavier after telling him that, because of what Dad taught me: the people you love are always going to let you down. "I feel you, Coach."

"How's summer school going?"

Another rocket comes his way. "A'right."

He hangs onto the ball. "I heard you're making friends with Tio Hudson. Is that right?"

I can't tell him the truth, which is exactly the opposite: I think I made an enemy in Tio since I didn't do what he asked about Bubble. Seems like proof I'm always gonna let somebody down. "Not really, he's just in summer school with me."

"What defines you, Xavier, is the people you hang out with, understand?"

He finally throws the ball back. I drop it.

Seems about right. Coach Baldwin says he wants me on his team, but what he don't know is that red road uniform ain't never gonna cover up the blue of Eliot and the one Dad wore in the federal pen.

"Throw me the ball, Xavier."

I pick the ball up, set up to throw, and it sails over his head, out of control.

33.

"Xavier, just listen to me. Think about what you're doing."

I sit with Mr. Big in the hallway, outside of Miss Williams's room. Something happened, but I'm blacking it out. It's kind of like I did about Dad's arrest. I was there; the sirens and screams in my dreams weren't nightmares but memories. Maybe he could've gotten away, but he didn't because he protected me. And how do I repay him? Everything is my fault. It's on me.

"You can't talk to a teacher that way," Mr. Big says, softly. I don't break my stare.

"I just don't care," I say it once and then ten more times. "I'm leaving. I'm done. Out."

"Xavier, if you walk out that front door, we'll need to suspend you," he says, still soft, like talking quietly is going calm me down. I have *The Red Badge of Courage* in my hand.

"I don't care," I say. Except the truth is probably I care too much. I'm angry at Dad, but then I'm angry with myself for being angry with him. I'm the failure, not him. I'm a little man, not a real one. I'm nothing and gonna be nothing. I rip the cover off the book and throw it. "I don't care."

"If we suspend you from summer school, you'll need to repeat tenth grade."

I rip more pages from the book, and then I tear the ripped out pages into shreds.

"I'm just telling you your options," Mr. Big says. He puts his hand on my shoulder just like Coach Baldwin used to do, just like I dreamed of my dad doing all those years, except he was inside and I was locked out of his life. And when he came home, it was like I was expecting him to be some hero, like he'd get everything back to normal, except better. Some hero. Marcus was wrong: I *am* the villain. "Xavier, you need to go back inside and apologize to Miss Williams for what you said."

"No." I get up and start toward the exit, still tearing pages, faster and harder.

"Don't do this, Xavier," he yells.

I rip the rest of the book in half and hurl it at him. "Don't tell me what to do!"

Before he can say another word, my fists shut his mouth.

34.

"Horton, you have a visitor."

It's visiting time at Eliot. I've been here for two months and Mom comes every time; Dad still hasn't showed for any. Tomorrow I leave— for Westborough, the state juvenile correctional facility. A real prison like Dad was in, but for kids. It's not a matter of where I go, but how long. My lawyer thinks he can get it under a year. Whatever.

Mom comes into the mod, sits at the table, and yawns like any other Saturday morning. Except it's not. Westborough's not an easy haul from home, but I need her to visit. I don't want to come home in a year a stranger. I need Dad to visit too, but I can't ask him. I can't take hearing no as the answer.

"How are you doing?" Mom asks. I shrug; there's nothing to tell. Every day, it's stand in line, tuck in your shirt, count off, quiet in the hall, do as you're told. Inside, outside, it don't seem to matter. "Xavier, we need to talk about something."

"How's Dad?" I ask. I never ask why he doesn't come to visit. She shrugs.

"He's trying, Xavier, really trying, but it's hard, even for a strong man like your father."

Strong, weak, courage, coward, snitch, hero, father, son: all words I'm still sorting through for my dad and me.

"What do we need to talk about?" I ask.

Mom looks around the room. "I heard from a girl named Jennie. And her parents."

Sure, now she gets back in touch. Wonder if her folks found my old texts. "What about?"

Mom leans in toward me, like I was the only person in the world. "She's pregnant and says you're the dad. Is that true, Xavier? Is that really possible?"

My eyes drop and I can't get a noise out as the words sink in. Mom asks more questions, but I'm still working on the first one. I nod. Then we sit in silence as tears run down Mom's cheeks.

"So, what is it?" I finally ask. *It.* My child.

Mom pauses and wipes her tears. She puts her hand over her eyes like she was blinded, then looks at me straight and breathes deep. "A son."

AFTERWORD

As of 2014, it's estimated that more than 2.7 million children in the United States have a parent behind bars. About one in five of those kids are teenagers. While having parents in prison presents challenges at any age, it may be particularly hard for teenagers, as they try to find their way in the world.

The Locked Out series explores the realities of parental incarceration through the eyes of teens dealing with it. These stories are fictional, but the experiences that Patrick Jones writes about are daily life for many youths.

The characters deal with racism, stigma,

shame, sadness, confusion, and isolation—common struggles for children with parents in prison. Many teens are forced to move from their homes, schools, or communities as their families cope with their parents' incarcerations.

These extra challenges can affect teens with incarcerated parents in different ways. Kids often struggle in school—they are at increased risk for skipping school, feeling disconnected from classmates, and failing classes. They act out and test boundaries. And they're prone to taking risks, like using substances or engaging in other illegal activities.

In addition, studies have shown that youth involved in the juvenile justice system are far more likely than their peers to have a parent in the criminal justice system. In Minnesota, for example, boys in juvenile correctional facilities are ten times more likely than boys in public schools to have a parent currently incarcerated. This cycle of incarceration is likely caused by many factors. These include systemic differences in the distribution of wealth and resources, as well as bias within policies and practices.

The Locked Out series offers a glimpse into this complex world. While the books don't sugarcoat reality, each story offers a window of hope. The teen characters have a chance to thrive despite difficult circumstances.

These books highlight the positive forces that make a difference in teens' lives: a loving, consistent caregiver; other supportive, trustworthy adults; meaningful connections at school; and participation in sports or other community programs. Indeed, these are the factors in teens' lives that mentoring programs around the country aim to strengthen, along with federal initiatives such as My Brother's Keeper, launched by President Obama.

This series serves as a reminder that just because a parent is locked up, it doesn't mean kids need to be locked out.

—Dr. Rebecca Shlafer
Department of Pediatrics,
University of Minnesota

AUTHOR ACKNOWLEDGMENTS

Thanks to Dr. Rebecca J. Shlafer and members of her research team for reading and commenting on this manuscript. Also thanks to Raven, Ricardo, and Shayna from South St. Paul Community Learning Center, and Dan Marcou, for their manuscript reviews.

ABOUT THE AUTHOR

Patrick Jones is the author of more than twenty-five novels for teens. He has also written two nonfiction books about combat sports: *The Main Event*, on professional wrestling, and *Ultimate Fighting*, on mixed martial arts. He has spoken to students at more than one hundred alternative schools and has worked with incarcerated teens and adults for more than a decade. Find him on the web at www.connectingya.com and on Twitter: @PatrickJonesYA.

LOCKED OUT

RETURNING TO NORMAL

PATRICH JONES

TAKING SIDES

PATRICH JONES

GUARDING SECRETS

PATRICH JONES

RAISING HEAVEN

PATRICH JONES

DOING RIGHT

PATRICH JONES

CHECK OUT ALL OF THE TITLES IN THE LOCKED OUT SERIES